DUNSTON
Checks In

A novelization by Dinah Sawyer
Based on the screenplay by John Hopkins
and Bruce Graham
Story by John Hopkins
Directed by Ken Kwapis

A PARACHUTE PRESS BOOK

Dunston
CHECKS IN

TWENTIETH CENTURY FOX PRESENTS A JOE WIZAN / TODD BLACK PRODUCTION A KEN KWAPIS FILM JASON ALEXANDER "DUNSTON CHECKS IN" FAYE DUNAWAY
ERIC LLOYD RUPERT EVERETT GLENN SHADIX AND PAUL REUBENS MUSIC BY MILES GOODMAN EDITED BY JON POLL PRODUCTION DESIGNER RUSTY SMITH DIRECTOR OF PHOTOGRAPHY PETER COLLISTER
EXECUTIVE PRODUCER RODNEY LIBER PRODUCED BY TODD BLACK AND JOE WIZAN SCREENPLAY BY JOHN HOPKINS AND BRUCE GRAHAM STORY BY JOHN HOPKINS DIRECTED BY KEN KWAPIS

A PARACHUTE PRESS BOOK
Parachute Press, Inc.
156 Fifth Avenue
New York, NY 10010

Printed in the U.S.A.
January 1996
ISBN: 0-938753-94-0
10 9 8 7 6 5 4 3 2 1

CHAPTER 1

"I'm looking for a target," Kyle Grant whispered into his walkie-talkie.

Eleven-year-old Kyle was crouched on a balcony. It overlooked the lobby of the Majestic Hotel in New York City. Kyle peered down at the wealthy guests as they wandered through the lobby. Several of them stopped to stare at the marble fountain in the center of the room. The fountain was gigantic! A statue of Cupid gently spurted water out of its mouth into a large round pool.

Kyle's fourteen-year-old brother, Brian, was at the other end of the walkie-talkie. Brian was in the hotel's boiler room, way down in the basement.

"Stay focused, Kyle," Brian's voice crackled through the walkie-talkie. He had his hand on a valve marked FOUNTAIN PRESSURE. "We're on a mission."

Kyle and Brian lived at the Majestic Hotel. But they weren't guests. They lived there because their father, Mr. Robert Grant, was the hotel manager. Their mother had died several years before. And their father was a very busy man. So lots of times Kyle and Brian had to spend the afternoons by themselves. That's what they were doing at this very moment.

Kyle looked around the lobby. He spotted Norm picking on Artie—as usual. Artie was Kyle's favorite bellman. He had worked at the Majestic Hotel for years. Norm was Artie's boss. And he was always mean. Artie knew how to handle it, though. He *always* kept his eyes on the floor. He *never* looked up. That way Norm could never tell if Artie was upset.

"Hey, Brian?" Kyle said into the walkie-talkie. "Norm. Norm is our target."

"Just say the word," Brian replied.

"Wait," Kyle said. "A guest is standing with Norm. Wow! She's got six huge suitcases!"

Kyle saw that Norm was ordering poor Artie to carry *all* the suitcases. Okay, Norm, he thought. You're going to get it!

The lady stepped away from Norm.

"Ready," Kyle told Brian. "Get set . . ."

In the boiler room Brian turned the water-pressure valve a tiny bit.

The Cupid statue gave a little burp.

"Hold it, Brian," ordered Kyle. "Another guest is in the way. I don't want to hit him—he's carrying a cute dog."

Kyle watched as the guest—a big guy with glasses—passed the fountain. His fluffy little dog growled at Norm.

Kyle smiled. Now he *really* liked that dog!

Norm leaned toward the Cupid. Kyle knew Norm was trying to find out why the statue had burped. Norm leaned even closer.

Perfect! thought Kyle. "Go!" he commanded.

Brian turned the fountain valve all the way up.

But it was too late. Norm had leaned over too far. He slipped! One of his arms plunged into the fountain. His feet slid out from under him. Norm fell to the floor as a huge jet of water exploded from Cupid's mouth.

Kyle gasped. The stream of water missed Norm. It sailed right over his head and hit the lady with the six suitcases! Kyle heard her shriek as she fought the spray. Just as she managed to get out of the way, the big man with glasses walked by.

The water slammed into him! He fell backward. The little dog went flying. The dog sailed through the air. It landed right on top of the lady. She was so surprised that she took a step back and fell over the edge of the fountain. Splash! She landed in the pool. The little dog fell with her.

Kyle covered his eyes. This plan wasn't working too well. Then he peeked through his fingers. The lady sat in the fountain, screaming at Norm. Kyle spotted the scruffy dog doing the dog paddle around the Cupid.

The man with glasses began calling the dog.

"Here, Neil!" he cried. "Come, baby!" He leaned forward to pull his dog from the fountain. Kyle saw that the lady thought he was trying to help her out of the water. She lunged for the big man, grabbing his arm. But she slipped on the wet marble and toppled back into the fountain. She pulled the man in with her!

Kyle groaned. He hoped his father wasn't anywhere near the lobby. Mr. Grant didn't like it when the guests got upset. "Brian?" he said into his walkie-talkie. "We, uh, hit some guests."

"Abandon mission!" Brian barked back. "Repeat, abandon mission!"

Kyle didn't have to be told twice. He jammed his walkie-talkie into his pocket and tucked his skateboard under his arm. He bolted down the back stairs three at a time. When he reached the ramp to the basement, Kyle hopped onto his skateboard. He began picking up speed. He'd almost reached the boiler room when he spotted Brian heading for him on his Rollerblades.

Kyle tried to slow down, but he was going too fast. He barreled down the ramp. He was heading straight for a cement wall!

Kyle was only an inch away from the wall when Brian's hand grabbed him and stopped him. Kyle breathed a sigh of relief. He could always count on Brian.

"Let's hide out till things calm down," Brian

suggested. He took off again. Kyle followed. He noticed that Brian wore nice clothes—a dress shirt and dark pants—with his Rollerblades and his helmet.

Kyle rolled his eyes. Even though both boys had brown hair and big brown eyes, they never looked like each other. That was because Brian always dressed up. He even combed his hair. Kyle didn't care much about his clothes. Or his hair.

The boys sailed down a hallway filled with crates of hotel soap, stacks of towels, and piles of paper towels. But Brian was bigger and faster. Kyle was afraid that he would be left behind. He reached out and grabbed his big brother's belt. Much better! Brian pulled him smoothly around the next curve.

"That's a real leather belt," Brian called over his shoulder. "Get your sweaty paws off!"

"Sorry!" Kyle cried. He let go of the belt as they headed for a stack of toilet paper. Big mistake! As Brian took the next corner, Kyle kept going straight.

A tower of toilet paper loomed before him. Kyle gulped. He couldn't stop! Kyle hit the stack of paper. He banged his nose on the wall behind the pile. Toilet-paper rolls showered down on his head.

For a moment Kyle lay still, buried in toilet paper. He was trapped! Then he cleared his throat. "Um, Brian?" he called. "Briaaaaan?"

CHAPTER 2

Brian held an ice pack to Kyle's nose. Kyle yelped as the cold ice touched his sore face.

The boys were hiding out in the hotel kitchen. But Kyle knew that sooner or later their father would find them. And he wouldn't be happy.

Mr. Grant pushed open the kitchen door. As always he wore an expensive blue suit. Not a hair on his head was out of place. Kyle's father usually had a smile on his face—especially when he was talking to a Majestic Hotel guest. But right now Mr. Grant looked angry.

"What have you two been—" Mr. Grant yelled.

Brian let the ice pack slip from Kyle's banged-up nose.

The angry look disappeared from Mr. Grant's face. "Kyle," he cried, kneeling beside his younger son. "Are you all right?"

Kyle nodded. Mr. Grant took the ice pack from Brian. He held it to Kyle's nose himself.

"It was Kyle's idea," Brian volunteered. "I'm like you, Dad. No imagination."

"We didn't mean to spray the guests, Dad," Kyle added.

"We were aiming for Norm," Brian explained. "He was picking on Artie again. And besides, he stole our Frisbee this morning."

"He didn't steal it," Mr. Grant replied. "He dug it out of the breakfast buffet where you two threw it." He shot Brian a look. "Is that my new belt you're wearing?"

"Yeah," answered Brian. "Nice, isn't it?"

Mr. Grant snapped his fingers. Brian began taking off his father's belt. Even though his face was sore, Kyle smiled.

Mr. Grant sighed. "Okay, let me drill something into your heads for I hope the last time," he said. "The Crystal Ball is this week. It is the biggest social event of the season. All the important people in New York will be there. Mr. and Mrs. Dubrow, I might remind you, own this hotel. They expect the ball to go off perfectly. *Perfectly.* And if it doesn't . . ."

"Will Mrs. Dubrow yell at you?" asked Kyle.

"He wouldn't be around long enough to get yelled at," Brian put in. "Mrs. Dubrow would *fire* him!"

"Very good," Mr. Grant said, looking pleased. "You're catching on. So unless you two want to move from a five-star hotel to a trailer park, we will have no more trouble. No more playing jokes on Norm. And no more soaking the guests."

Kyle and Brian nodded solemnly.

Mr. Grant smiled at them. "Next week, after the Crystal Ball is over," he said, *"we* go on vacation to Barbados for ten whole days. The three of us get to be the guests. We'll nag and complain and make other people's lives miserable for a change."

Kyle grinned. He liked the idea of *staying* in a hotel a lot more than living in one.

"But until then," Mr. Grant said sternly, "you're both grounded."

Barbados! Kyle could hardly wait. So what if he was grounded? That didn't stop him from pretending he was in Barbados already. He put on his swim trunks, face mask, and snorkel. Then he squeezed his feet into his flippers. *Swammmp. Swammmp.* Kyle loved the sound the flippers made on their living-room carpet!

He padded over to the big tropical-fish tank and squatted beside it. He pretended that he was swimming along with the fish. Now *this* was a vacation!

Kyle was really into his "snorkeling." He didn't hear his father call him for dinner. Suddenly a voice yelled in his ear: *"Kyle!"*

Kyle looked up at his father.

"What are you doing?" asked Mr. Grant.

Kyle stepped out from behind the fish tank. *Swammmp. Swammmp.* "Practicing," he answered. "For our trip to Barbados."

"Come on." His father smiled. "Time to eat."

At the dinner table Mr. Grant studied computer printouts. Brian read *The Wall Street Journal*. Kyle pushed food around on his plate.

"I figure we'll need spear guns for the sharks in Barbados, right?" Kyle asked. "Wouldn't it be cool to shoot a shark?"

"Don't even think about it," Mr. Grant replied without looking up.

"Will the hotel in Barbados have spear guns?" asked Kyle.

"I'll ask when we get there." Mr. Grant noticed Kyle's plate. "Don't you like your steak?" he asked.

Kyle thought about it. The steak was delicious. Everything the kitchen sent up to the Grants' apartment was delicious. In fact, almost every meal Kyle had ever eaten tasted wonderful. It was getting boring.

"It's okay," Kyle told his father.

"*Okay?*" cried Mr. Grant. "It's the best steak in the city!"

"Remember when we went to Aunt Lisa's?" Kyle asked. "And she made us steak?"

"That cheap piece of round steak? Overcooked and badly seasoned." Mr. Grant wrinkled his nose. "What about it?"

Kyle shrugged. "Well, I liked it. That's all."

At least it was something different, Kyle thought. I bet normal people eat like Aunt Lisa all the time.

"What are you saying, Kyle?" asked Mr. Grant. "You want me to ask Chef Bernard to overcook your dinner for you some night?"

Kyle didn't answer. He knew a chef could never cook the way Aunt Lisa did.

"Do you know how lucky we are?" Mr. Grant continued. "When I was a kid, I was lucky to get steak once a year."

"Maybe we could cook for ourselves one night," Kyle suggested. "We should learn how."

"Why?" Mr. Grant asked. "We have a five-star restaurant that will deliver to us twenty-four hours a day!"

"But what if we're in a plane crash on the way back from Barbados?" Kyle cried. "What if we're stranded in the jungle? We can use the spear guns to shoot food. But what if we don't know how to cook it?"

Mr. Grant laughed. "Kyle, you think just like your mother!" he said.

Kyle smiled. "That's good, right?"

"Yeah," Mr. Grant said quietly. "And it was never boring!"

Kyle was bored as he sat in the hotel lobby the next morning. There was never anything to do here—no other kids to play with, nowhere to run around. He couldn't wait until they left for Barbados!

But Kyle could tell that Brian wasn't bored. His brother was watching two pretty girls as they walked through the lobby. One had long brown hair. The other was blond. They both looked about eighteen years old.

"If you have to be grounded," Brian said happily, "a five-star hotel is the place to be."

"Those girls are too *old* for you!" Kyle pointed out.

Brian didn't answer. He stood up and went to talk to the girls.

Kyle rolled his eyes. He didn't think it would be any fun to talk to teenage girls. But it might be fun to check out the huge steamer trunk sitting by the reception desk. It was enormous! He hopped up and hurried over for a closer look.

The trunk was plastered with colorful stickers from all over the world. Someday I'm going to visit all of these places, Kyle thought excitedly. First Barbados, and then the whole rest of the world! And I'm not staying in any five-star hotels, either!

He bent closer to examine the stickers. He looked at all the stickers on one side of the trunk. Then he walked slowly around to the other side. He had never even heard of so many countries. Kyle reached out and traced one sticker—from

Africa! As he touched the trunk Kyle felt a movement. He drew back quickly.

Something was *moving* inside that trunk!

Cautiously Kyle raised his fist. He knocked softly on the trunk. And something knocked back! Kyle couldn't believe it. He stared at the trunk for a moment. Then he decided to knock again. He reached forward . . .

Whack! A loud cracking sound split the air as a walking stick hit the trunk. It barely missed Kyle's fingers. Surprised, he jumped away.

"Terribly sorry," said a voice with an English accent.

Kyle stared up at a tall man. He saw that the man was wearing a fancy suit. And he was smiling. But Kyle didn't like his smile—it didn't seem like a happy smile. Kyle thought this man looked mean.

The man patted his walking stick. "It slipped out of my hand," he explained.

No way, thought Kyle. He did it on purpose! He tried to hit me! "I . . . I heard something in the trunk," Kyle stammered.

"Like to see a trick?" the man asked, changing the subject. He reached behind Kyle's ear and pulled out a silver dollar. Kyle smiled even though the man still looked mean. His dad said he should always be polite to guests of the Majestic.

"I can do all sorts of tricks," the man said.

Leaning close to Kyle, he whispered, "My specialty is making nosy little boys disappear."

Kyle didn't know what to say—no grownup had ever been so nasty to him before! I don't like this guy, Kyle thought. I bet he's keeping a little boy in that trunk!

Kyle backed up some more.

The tall man turned away. He spoke to the desk clerk. "My name is Rutledge," Kyle heard him say.

"Good afternoon, Mr. Rutledge," said the clerk.

"That's *Lord* Rutledge," the tall man snapped.

This guy isn't nice to anybody, Kyle said to himself. He gazed around the lobby, hoping to see Brian. Instead he saw a pretty woman wearing a big diamond necklace. She rushed up to Lord Rutledge and began talking to him.

"Ah, Mrs. Dellacroce!" cried Lord Rutledge. He kissed the lady on the cheek.

I guess Lord Rutledge can be friendly after all, Kyle realized. The Englishman was smiling widely as he spoke to the woman. But Kyle noticed that he kept staring at her necklace.

At least he isn't looking at *me* anymore! Kyle thought. He snuck away from the nasty Englishman.

Kyle hurried toward his father's office. He had to tell his dad about this mean Rutledge guy. And about the mysterious knocking inside his trunk!

CHAPTER 3

"Dad!" called Kyle as he burst through the office door. "There's this weird guy checking in! He's got a huge trunk."

Kyle's father gave a small groan.

"I knocked on his trunk," Kyle said. "And it *knocked back*!"

Just then Mr. Grant's phone rang. He picked it up.

While his father took the call, Kyle looked around the office. There were lots of napkins on his dad's desk. They were folded in all different ways. Kyle figured his father had been trying out table settings for the big Crystal Ball. Nobody in the whole hotel seemed interested in anything these days but that stupid ball!

"Thanks for the warning," Mr. Grant said. He hung up.

Finally! thought Kyle. "His name's Rutledge," Kyle continued. "Lord Rutledge. He has an English accent. And he's probably a kidnapper!"

But Mr. Grant didn't call security. Instead he quickly stood up from behind his desk. He hurried Kyle to the door.

"The front desk just called," his father explained. "Mr. and Mrs. Dubrow are on their way to see me. *Now.*"

Kyle gasped. He didn't like the Majestic Hotel very much. And he definitely didn't like his dad being so busy all the time. But even Kyle knew how important the Dubrows were. They owned the whole hotel! They were the only people in the world who could tell his dad what to do.

And they were scary!

Kyle didn't mind Mr. Dubrow. He seemed like a pretty nice old guy—kind of like a grandpa. Mrs. Dubrow was the really scary one. She wasn't nearly as old as Mr. Dubrow. And she was always yelling. She even yelled at Kyle's dad sometimes. Kyle didn't like her. He didn't think anyone liked her.

Kyle stopped in the doorway of his father's office. The Dubrows were marching through the lobby. Kyle was amazed to see how fast Mrs. Dubrow was walking in her six-inch high heels. She was halfway to the office!

It was too late for Kyle to escape. He and his dad watched as Consuelo—one of the hotel housekeepers—rounded a hallway corner. Kyle liked Consuelo. She always gave him mints that were supposed to be left on guests' pillows. And now she was carrying the little dog that had fallen into the fountain. But Consuelo was so busy talking to the dog that she didn't notice the Dubrows heading straight for her. She bumped right into the hotel owners.

"Oh, no!" moaned Mr. Grant. "I don't need this."

Poor Consuelo! thought Kyle. The housekeeper was trying to apologize to the Dubrows. But the dog wasn't apologizing. He was barking like crazy. He snapped at Mrs. Dubrow! Kyle tried not to giggle.

Kyle watched Mrs. Dubrow brush herself off. Then she glanced at Consuelo's name tag. She grabbed her husband's elbow and yanked him toward Mr. Grant's office.

"Quick," Mr. Grant whispered. "Hide under the desk!"

Kyle dove under his father's big desk. His father's knees jabbed him in the back as he sat down. But Kyle didn't mind. It was kind of fun hiding from the Dubrows. He would get to hear everything they said.

"Robert," Mrs. Dubrow said. "How nice to see you."

"Mrs. Dubrow! What a pleasant surprise," said Mr. Grant.

Yeah, right! thought Kyle.

"Have you been reading the guest-survey cards, Robert?" Mr. Dubrow asked. "You've got to keep up on them—that's how you know what our guests want. Do you know what they want? Fluffy towels, Robert! Nice fluffy towels!"

"I'll speak to the laundry about it," Mr. Grant assured him.

"Victor," Mrs. Dubrow cut in. "Why don't you sit over there and read your cards?"

"Yes, dear," answered her husband. Kyle saw Mr. Dubrow's feet shuffling toward the couch.

"Robert," Mrs. Dubrow said, "we have always been proud of the Majestic Hotel's five-star rating."

"Five stars is as good as it gets," Kyle's dad agreed.

"Not anymore," Mrs. Dubrow said. "The hotel-rating people have decided to award a *sixth* star to the world's best hotels."

"Large soap!" Mr. Dubrow shouted from the couch. Kyle figured the old man must still be reading the guest surveys. "That'll get you a sixth star!" Mr. Dubrow bellowed.

"Yes, dear," Mrs. Dubrow answered impatiently. "Robert, I hear that they've sent a spy here to rate the Majestic Hotel."

Kyle's dad gasped. "There's a hotel-rating person *here*? *Now?*" he asked.

"Of course someone is here now!" Mrs. Dubrow answered. "The Crystal Ball is coming up. It's the social event of the season." She paused. "I want to win a sixth star, Robert. I will

19

be very upset if I don't get it."

"I understand," Mr. Grant said. Kyle wondered why his father sounded so worried.

"Wonderful," said Mrs. Dubrow. "And next week, when the ball is over and we are a *six*-star hotel, every travel section in the country will interview us. I want *you* in the pictures with me, Robert."

"Sorry," said Mr. Grant. "I'm on vacation next week."

"Don't even think about going on vacation," Mrs. Dubrow replied.

"No!" Kyle yelped. He bolted up, banging his head on the desk.

"Ow! I knocked my knee," his father said quickly. He darted a look at Kyle under the desk. The look said, *Not now, Kyle!*

"But Dad!" Kyle whispered.

"I need you here," Mrs. Dubrow was saying.

"Dad, you promised!" Kyle whispered urgently.

"Robert!" Mrs. Dubrow snapped. "What is your problem?"

"Nothing!" answered Mr. Grant.

"Then why do you seem to be talking to your lap?" Mrs. Dubrow demanded.

Mr. Grant gazed at Kyle again. Then he said, "Well, Mrs. Dubrow, this is the second time I've had to cancel my vacation . . ."

"Third!" Kyle whispered. "It's the third time!"

Suddenly Kyle saw a bunch of papers flutter off his father's desk. The next thing he knew his father was bending over to get them. His face came within inches of Kyle's.

"Don't let her ruin it, Dad!" Kyle begged.

"I'll take care of it!" Mr. Grant whispered. "Just clam up!" Mr. Grant sat up straight. "Mrs. Dubrow," he said, "I promised my sons—"

"Robert, let me put it this way," Mrs. Dubrow interrupted him. "If the Crystal Ball is a big success, the Majestic Hotel will get a sixth star. Then you can take your sons on a fabulous vacation . . . eventually. But if we *don't* get a sixth star, time off won't be a problem. Because you'll have *plenty* of it."

Kyle knew what that meant. If his father didn't do what Mrs. Dubrow wanted, she would fire him. Kyle knew his dad didn't want that to happen.

Kyle sighed. Mr. Grant didn't say a word.

"I'm glad that's settled," Mrs. Dubrow continued. "Oh, and there's a guest here . . . Lord Somebody. I think he might be the spy that the rating people sent. Find out."

"I'll try," answered Kyle's father.

Kyle watched Mrs. Dubrow's feet head for the door.

"Oh, Robert. One more thing," she said from the doorway. "I want you to fire someone. It keeps the staff on their toes. I haven't asked you to fire anyone since . . ."

"Since Christmas," Mr. Grant finished for her.

"Right. Fire that clumsy housekeeper," said Mrs. Dubrow. "Connie. No . . . Constance. No . . . Consuelo! The one who nearly knocked me down before. Fire her immediately."

Kyle heard Mrs. Dubrow snap her fingers. Mr. Dubrow stood up and followed his wife out the door.

Kyle crawled out from under the desk. "That's not fair, Dad!" he exclaimed. "You promised—"

"Let me work on it," said his father. Mr. Grant picked up his phone. "Send in Consuelo," he said.

Kyle was surprised. "But you can't fire Consuelo!" he protested.

"Don't worry," Mr. Grant told him. "Mrs. Dubrow never remembers who she wants me to fire. Watch this!"

Consuelo slowly opened the door.

"Ah, Consuelo," Mr. Grant said. "Come in, come in. As of right now, I'm giving you a week's paid vacation."

Consuelo's face lit up.

"On one condition," added Mr. Grant. "You have to run out of this office crying."

Kyle and Mr. Grant watched from the doorway as Consuelo ran out in a flood of tears. In the lobby Kyle spotted Mrs. Dubrow watching Consuelo too. She seemed to enjoy every tear.

Kyle liked fooling Mrs. Dubrow. But he was still upset about their vacation. How could they cancel a trip to Barbados?

"Dad—" Kyle began.

"Wait a second." Mr. Grant checked his appointment calendar. Kyle was itching to talk to his dad. Maybe he should make an appointment. Maybe then he'd get a chance. He watched as his dad opened his desk drawer and pulled out . . . a Frisbee.

Kyle grinned. "Hey! Can we go to the park?"

"Not exactly," said his dad. "Come on." He put an arm around Kyle's shoulders and gave him a squeeze.

Kyle followed his father to the Majestic Hotel's ballroom. All the tables and chairs were stacked against the walls. The enormous empty space was perfect for a game of Frisbee!

Mr. Grant was wearing a suit. He had to keep his clothes neat. And the cellular phone in his pocket kept ringing. Mr. Grant had to answer the phone with one hand while he threw the Frisbee with the other.

Even so, Kyle thought his dad played pretty well.

CHAPTER 4

While Kyle and his dad played Frisbee in the ballroom, Lord Rutledge was unpacking in his hotel room. He hooked up his laptop computer to the hotel's phone jack. Then he broke into the hotel computer. He called up a list of hotel guests.

"How about a little 'practice round' before the Crystal Ball?" he said. He didn't have an English accent anymore. "Ah, Mrs. Dellacroce. I remember you—and your diamond necklace. Hmmm. Room 812."

Rutledge pulled a small key from his pocket. He looked at the key and smiled. Then he crossed the room to his trunk. It was the big, colorful trunk that Kyle had knocked on—the trunk that had *knocked back*. Rutledge bent down and used his key to unlock the trunk.

"Let's get to work," he said.

A long, hairy arm came out of the trunk. Then another. And then a large, round face. A face covered in orange hair. The face of an orangutan.

The orangutan smiled. He was happy to be out of that dark trunk. He let out a cheerful gurgle. Then he shot out a hand and snatched a pen from Rutledge's desk. He stuck the pen between his teeth.

Rutledge snatched the pen back. "Monkey spit," he commented, wiping it off. He grabbed the orangutan's arm. "I need you, Dunston," he said. *"For the moment.* But don't push me!"

Rutledge angrily stomped into the bathroom.

Dunston scampered over to Rutledge's desk chair. He sat down and put his feet up on the desk.

A few minutes later Rutledge came out of the bathroom. He was dressed as a Majestic Hotel bellman. Dunston knew what that meant! Whenever Rutledge dressed up in a funny outfit, Dunston had to go to work. Dunston didn't mind. Sometimes work was fun!

Dunston watched as Rutledge looked into a mirror. The orangutan hopped up from the desk chair. He scrambled over to where Rutledge was standing. Rutledge slicked back his hair. Dunston pretended to slick back his hair. Rutledge put on a bellman's hat. Dunston grabbed the ice bucket from the chest of drawers. He put it on his head, hooting merrily.

"You think you're funny, don't you, Dunston?" asked Rutledge. He put on a pair of glasses.

Dunston grinned. He began drumming on his ice-bucket hat. "I need that!" Rutledge yelled. He whisked the bucket off the orangutan's head.

Then he pulled a scrap of red fabric out of his pocket. "I'm going to mark the window for tonight," Rutledge told Dunston. "When you go to work, you have to look for this." He held the fabric out to Dunston.

The orangutan reached for the pretty red flag. Rutledge snatched it away. "Just remember it!" he snapped.

Dunston stuck out his tongue. He blew a loud raspberry.

"That's disgusting, Dunston," said Rutledge. He pointed to the trunk. "Okay, back into your room."

Dunston shook his head no.

"I don't want any attitude. Move!"

Dunston shook his head even harder: *NO!*

"All right. Have it your way." Rutledge turned around.

Dunston smiled. This was more like it. He didn't want to go back into that old cramped trunk. He wanted to stay out in the big hotel room. He did a little dance to celebrate—he didn't usually get his way!

Dunston was so busy dancing that he didn't see Rutledge twist the handle on his walking stick. He didn't see the small whip hidden inside the stick.

Suddenly Rutledge whirled around and cracked the whip at Dunston's feet. It made a sharp, loud snapping sound. Dunston jumped. He was scared!

With a whimper he scurried back into the trunk. Rutledge slammed it shut.

Mr. Grant had to go back to his office after the Frisbee game. Kyle ran down to the hotel security room. He still wanted to find out about that knocking trunk! When Kyle reached the security room, Brian was already there. He and Murray, the hotel security chief, were scanning a dozen TV monitors that showed what was going on all over the Majestic Hotel. They were looking for anyone who was doing something wrong.

Kyle began describing Lord Rutledge to them. "He's a really mean, scary-looking guy," he said. "With an English accent."

But Kyle could tell that Brian and Murray were only half listening. Their eyes were glued to the monitors. Kyle sighed. He never understood why his brother liked the hotel business so much. I guess he wants to be like Dad when he grows up, thought Kyle.

"Anyway, Murray," Kyle continued, "Lord Rutledge has a huge trunk with lots of stickers on it."

"Right," said Murray. His eyes never left the TV screen. "Scary guy. Huge trunk. Stickers. Got it."

Kyle had a feeling that Murray wouldn't

remember to look out for Lord Rutledge. He decided to look himself. He glanced at monitor six and saw a bellman with an ice bucket walking down a hallway. Kyle didn't recognize him. But there were lots of bellmen at the Majestic Hotel. This one was probably new.

Kyle watched as the bellman stopped at room 812. "Room service," he announced. He had a southern accent. Kyle giggled. There weren't many bellmen in New York City with southern accents.

Kyle glanced over at another monitor. So he didn't see the bellman put the ice bucket in front of the doorknob to shield it from the video camera. He didn't see him quickly pick the lock and sneak into the room.

"How's your lobster, Kyle?" Mr. Grant asked. It was dinnertime, and Kyle still felt sad about their canceled vacation.

Kyle shrugged.

"I had Chef Bernard overcook it. He even kicked it across the floor a couple of times," Mr. Grant joked.

Kyle didn't crack a smile.

"Lighten up, Kyle," said Brian. "The Majestic Hotel is paradise. What do you need to go on vacation for?"

Kyle thought maybe he'd make Brian a list.

TOP TEN REASONS WHY I, KYLE GRANT, NEED TO GO ON VACATION: *#1—So I can get out of this boring old hotel.*

"I love the hotel," Brian went on. "In fact, I love the whole hotel business. It's so full of opportunity."

"Okay, Brian," said Mr. Grant, checking his calendar. "I'll give you an opportunity. You can walk Mr. Spalding's dog tonight at nine o'clock. Mr. Spalding is in room 408."

"No way!" Brian objected.

Kyle thought about that little dog. He smiled, remembering the way it had snapped at Mrs. Dubrow. What a good dog!

After dinner Kyle took the elevator down to the lobby. He sat on a chair beside a potted palm tree. He pretended to read a newspaper. But he secretly looked around for Lord Rutledge.

It didn't take long to find the Englishman. Kyle spotted him standing in the hotel lounge, talking to some other guests. But Kyle noticed that he kept glancing out into the lobby. He seemed to be looking for someone. Frowning, Kyle glanced around the lobby too. There was nobody in sight. When he looked into the lounge again, Kyle saw his father. Yikes! Mr. Grant shook hands with Lord Rutledge! Kyle raised his newspaper. He kept it up in front of his face for a long time. If his dad caught him spying on a hotel guest, he'd be in big trouble!

After a long time Kyle peeked out from behind his newspaper. He saw a woman wearing a fancy sequined dress. It was Mrs. Dellacroce, Kyle realized. She had been talking to Lord Rutledge the other day.

Quickly Kyle glanced into the lounge. He noticed that Lord Rutledge was staring at Mrs. Dellacroce as she left the hotel. Then he followed her outside.

Kyle ran over to the front window and peered out. Mrs. Dellacroce climbed into a taxi. He watched it drive away from the hotel.

Lord Rutledge stood outside the hotel door. He watched the taxi too. Then he pulled a beeper from his pocket and tossed it in the air with a big smile. He caught the beeper and climbed into another taxi. Kyle watched as he sped away.

Kyle frowned. He and Brian carried beepers. That was how their dad let them know when he wanted them. But why does Lord Rutledge have one? Kyle wondered. Who's he going to beep?

CHAPTER 5

Dunston was glad when Rutledge left for the evening. He liked having the hotel room to himself. It was much bigger than his tiny trunk!

As soon as Rutledge walked out, the orangutan lifted up the bedside lamp. There was the key he wanted—right where Rutledge had hidden it. Dunston scampered over to the mini-bar, near the bathroom. He used the key to unlock it. He took candy bars, a bag of chips, and a large lemonade over to the couch. Yum! Dunston had a feast!

Then he picked up the TV remote. He was in the mood for some serious channel surfing. He switched the channels, pointing and laughing at the shows he liked. Suddenly he stopped changing channels. His all-time favorite movie was on— *Planet of the Apes*. Forget channel surfing! The orangutan settled down to watch the whole movie.

But *Planet of the Apes* had barely started when Dunston's beeper went off. It was time to go to work.

Dunston rose slowly from the couch. He

turned off the TV. He stuffed candy wrappers and the empty chip bag back into the mini-bar. Then he took a black ninja outfit from the closet and put it on. He fastened a fanny pack around his waist. He put on a miner's hat with a light on the front.

He was ready.

Dunston pushed open the window. Then he climbed outside!

Meanwhile Brian stuffed a dollar bill into Kyle's shirt pocket. "Thanks for walking the dog for me, Kyle," he said. "Mr. Spalding is in room 408," he went on. "And don't forget to wait for the tip this time. We'll split it."

No problem, Kyle thought as he took the elevator to the fourth floor. He wasn't doing Brian's job because he wanted money. He was doing it because he liked dogs.

Kyle knocked on the door of room 408. Mr. Spalding answered. Kyle remembered what the big man had looked like sitting in the fountain. He tried not to laugh.

"I'm here to walk your dog," he told Mr. Spalding.

"His name is Neil," Mr. Spalding said. "After Neil Armstrong, the first man to walk on the moon." He handed the dog to Kyle. "Take good care of him. He's my pride and joy."

32

"I will," Kyle assured him.

Carefully Kyle carried Neil to the elevator. Mr. Spalding waved and closed his door. Then Kyle put Neil down on the floor.

"Okay, Neil," he said. "Let's have some fun!" He sat on the floor and rolled around with the dog. Neil jumped around him, playing and licking his face.

The boy and the dog were far too busy to glance out the hallway window. If they had looked, they would have seen a large, round, mysterious face peering in at them. Dunston's face.

Dunston had shimmied up a drain-pipe on the outside of the hotel. He climbed easily along the window ledges. The height didn't scare him at all. In fact, Dunston liked being high up—it reminded him of climbing trees. Rutledge never let him climb trees anymore.

Dunston was searching for a certain window. One with a red ribbon hanging out. But as he passed the hallway window, he noticed Kyle and Neil. He stopped climbing and watched them for a while. Dunston smiled. That boy really knew how to treat an animal! He watched them playing until the elevator came.

"Come on, boy!" Kyle crooned. "We're going up. Wait till you see the Majestic Hotel's famous rooftop dog-walking terrace!"

The boy and the dog disappeared into the

elevator. Dunston sighed. He wished he had a nice boy like that.

Then Dunston continued his search. There it was—the red ribbon! Quickly Dunston scaled the drainpipe. He opened the ribbon-marked window and hoisted himself inside. The room was dark, so he switched on his miner's-hat light. He directed the beam around the room.

Suddenly Dunston stopped. The beam of light had landed on something shiny. A diamond watch. Rutledge would like that, Dunston thought. Rutledge liked shiny things.

Dunston picked up the watch and stuffed it into his fanny pack. Then he looked around again. But this time he was looking for a radio. Dunston liked to listen to music while he worked. He turned the dials on the clock radio until loud music blared out. Then he began boogying around the room! Dunston looked for shiny things: silver coins, gold bracelets, a diamond pin, a stick of gum wrapped in silver foil, the shiny glass knob of the dresser drawer.

At last Dunston didn't see a single shiny thing left. Now came the fun part of his work—trashing the room!

Dunston grabbed an orange from a fruit basket. He held it in his hand and wound up like a major-league pitcher. He fired it. Bingo! It toppled a lamp. Dunston hooted and jumped up and down.

Next Dunston found a wide-brimmed hat and a scarf in the closet. He loved dressing up! He put them on. Then he continued to make a mess of the room. At last it looked just right. It looked like it had been searched by professional burglars.

Finally Dunston was finished. He took off his dress-up clothes. He climbed back out the window, shutting it behind him. He took the red ribbon off the window and put it in his fanny pack.

Dunston was about to climb down the drainpipe again when he heard a dog yapping. The sound came from the roof. Curious, Dunston shimmied up the pipe. He hopped up onto a ledge directly beneath the roof.

Kyle had been running Neil back and forth on his leash. Neil was yapping and having a great time. But all of a sudden the little dog stopped. He sniffed the air.

"What do you smell, boy?" asked Kyle. He could see that something was scaring the dog. Neil trembled and whimpered. He hid behind Kyle's legs. Kyle looked around, but the roof was empty.

Then Neil bolted, yanking the leash out of Kyle's hand.

"Hey!" Kyle dove for the leash. He belly flopped onto the gravel rooftop. But he was too late! The leash slithered away after Neil. Kyle looked up just in time to see Neil leap off the roof.

"No! Neil!" cried Kyle. He scrambled to his feet and rushed to the ledge. "Neil?" he called. Bravely he peered over the wall at the edge of the roof. He looked down into the alley that ran behind the Majestic Hotel. Kyle held his breath. Then he heard a sharp yapping from below. Kyle smiled. Neil was alive!

Kyle stood on tiptoe and peered farther over the wall. He tried to see exactly where Neil had fallen. Suddenly a bright light flashed in his eyes. Kyle blinked in surprise. Then he saw a round, hairy face pop up from the ledge below the roof!

Kyle gasped. How could someone be on that ledge? The face kept coming closer . . . and closer . . . and then it gave Kyle a big, sloppy kiss.

"Ugh!" yelled Kyle. He staggered backward, wiping his face. There was a monster on the roof! A hairy monster with gross slobbery kisses!

Kyle ran.

The monster was after him!

CHAPTER 6

When Kyle reached the door to the roof garden, he stopped. He glanced over his shoulder.

No monster.

Kyle looked around the roof.

Empty.

Cautiously he walked back to the wall at the edge of the roof. He heard Neil barking. I know I saw a monster, Kyle thought. I have monster spit all over me!

Kyle took a deep breath. The monster had been on the ledge beneath the roof. Would it still be there? He leaned over the wall again.

The monster was gone. Kyle stared at the side of the Majestic Hotel. Where was the monster? Suddenly he noticed something moving in the garbage dumpster down in the alley. Kyle squinted at it. Neil!

"Neil!" cried Mr. Spalding when Kyle brought him his dog.

The dog shivered in Kyle's arms. Bits of food and coffee grounds and other garbage clung to his fur. But he wasn't hurt. He licked Kyle's face.

"What happened?" cried Mr. Spalding. He grabbed Neil from Kyle and stared in horror at the little dog. "Neil is covered in . . . in *garbage!*" he yelled. He glanced at Kyle. "What are you waiting for?"

"A tip," Kyle answered. After all, Brian had told him to stay until he got a tip.

"You have a loooong wait!" Mr. Spalding told him. He slammed the door in Kyle's face.

By the time Kyle reached his apartment, Mr. Spalding had phoned his father. Kyle took a seat beside Brian on the couch. Their dad paced up and down as he spoke.

"Kyle," said Mr. Grant. "I know you're upset about our vacation being canceled. But that's no reason to *throw a guest's dog into the garbage!*"

"I didn't throw him into the garbage," protested Kyle.

"Well, what happened?" his father yelled.

"He jumped off the dog walk," Kyle explained.

"Why would a dog do that?" asked Mr. Grant. "Why?"

"Because he smelled the monster on the ledge," said Kyle.

"The monster on the ledge," Mr. Grant muttered. He took a deep breath. Kyle could tell his dad was trying to stay calm.

Brian nudged Kyle with his elbow. "Way to blow a tip, psycho," he teased.

Mr. Grant glared at his older son. "*You* were in charge of walking that dog," he scolded. Then he turned to Kyle. "Okay," he said. "Start at the beginning." He sipped a cup of tea while he listened to Kyle's story.

At last Kyle finished. Mr. Grant gazed at him for a long time. And Kyle knew his dad didn't believe there was a monster on the roof.

"Well," Mr. Grant said finally, "I'm going to pass sentence on you two. Brian, no videos and no using the security room to spy on the guests."

Brian groaned.

"Kyle—" began Mr. Grant. His voice was cut off by the ringing of the phone. Mr. Grant picked it up. "Yes?" he said. "What? Mrs. Dellacroce's room? *Robbed?*"

Dunston was looking fondly at a photograph taped inside his trunk. It showed Rutledge with his arms around a pair of orangutans. Both orangutans wore T-shirts. One shirt read DUNSTON, and the other read SAMSON. Along the top of the photo was a caption: O'MALLEY'S ORIGINAL ORANGUTANS!

With his finger Dunston gently petted the picture of Samson.

A key clicked in the lock on the hotel room door. Dunston glanced up as Rutledge came in and headed straight for the telephone.

"Room service?" he said. "I'd like a bottle of champagne and a fruit salad with extra bananas. Yes, bananas." He hung up and turned to Dunston. "Show me what you've got," he ordered.

Dunston zipped open the fanny pack. He pulled out a foil-wrapped stick of gum. Then he held it up and smiled at Rutledge.

"I am *not* amused!" shouted Rutledge, grabbing for the fanny pack.

Playfully Dunston dodged away. He leaped up on top of a tall chest of drawers.

"I'm in no mood for this!" yelled Rutledge. He picked up the riding whip and snapped it at Dunston.

Dunston hated that whip! He reached into the pack again and pulled out what looked like a huge diamond. Rutledge gasped. Then he saw what it was—the knob from a dresser drawer!

"Dunston, don't do this," warned Rutledge. "Remember what happened to your brother."

At the word *brother,* Dunston froze. He was frightened now.

"Samson liked to play games," Rutledge continued. "You don't want to end up like Samson when this job is over, do you?"

Dunston shook his head. He was afraid of Rutledge. But he was angry, too. Rutledge moved in on him, waving the whip.

Dunston wound up like a major-league pitcher.

He hurled the dresser knob. Bam! It bounced off Rutledge's forehead.

Rutledge reeled back. Dunston shrieked with laughter. Rutledge deserved that! But then Rutledge grabbed his walking stick. He flicked a trigger in the handle. A nasty pair of pinchers sprang out from the tip.

"Time for bed . . ." Rutledge said, aiming the pinchers at Dunston.

Dunston had had enough! He leaped off the chest of drawers. He hit Rutledge in the stomach, and they both fell over backward. The walking stick went flying. Dunston scooted away as Rutledge stumbled to his feet.

"It's discipline time, you little beast," growled Rutledge.

He picked up his stick. But Dunston was gone.

Rutledge checked under the bed. No Dunston. He prowled around the hotel room, searching. At last he spotted the open window. He rushed over and stuck out his head. "Dunston?" he called. "Daddy's sorry . . ."

Dunston was sitting happily on the ledge outside the window. He stuck out his tongue at "Daddy."

"Come back inside," Rutledge coaxed. "I'll give you bananas!"

But Dunston wasn't buying it. He knew if he went back inside, Rutledge would be mad again.

41

He would lock Dunston up in his trunk all night long. Dunston stood up on the ledge and shook his fist at Rutledge.

"Don't you threaten me!" shouted Rutledge. Angry, he started to climb out the window. Dunston shimmied quickly up a drainpipe. He left Rutledge halfway out on the ledge, calling into the night: "Dunston! Dunstooooon!"

Dunston smiled. He was free! He didn't need Rutledge. He would find a place to make a nice, soft nest. He could find snacks, too. He could find everything he needed. And he would never have to sleep in the trunk anymore. Or be afraid of that whip!

Dunston dashed across the roof of the hotel. He found an opening in the air-conditioning vent. Perfect! He slipped inside.

Kyle lay in bed, holding his old stuffed dog. The overhead light was blazing. But he didn't want to turn it off. He didn't want to be alone in the dark.

It was late when he heard his father let himself into the apartment. Mr. Grant had been out all evening, dealing with the police about Mrs. Dellacroce's stolen jewels. Now he tiptoed into Kyle's room and switched off the light.

Kyle bolted upright. "Leave it on!" he cried.

His father switched on the light again.

Kyle smiled and settled down in bed. " 'Night, Dad," he said. Then he turned to a photograph on his bedside table. It showed him standing on a beach next to his mother. " 'Night, Mom," he added.

Mr. Grant smiled. "Hey, you still say good night to Mom?"

"Yeah," said Kyle. "That's not stupid or anything, is it?"

"No." His father shook his head. "I do too."

At last Kyle closed his eyes and fell asleep. He felt safer with his dad home. But in the middle of the night Kyle woke up again. He stumbled out of bed and carried his stuffed dog under one arm as he headed for the bathroom.

Dunston had been traveling all over the hotel inside the air-conditioning vents. He was getting tired—and hungry! He wondered if he should go back to Rutledge's room. He would get in trouble, but at least Rutledge would probably give him bananas. Dunston glanced down at his fanny pack. He was glad that he had all the shiny things with him. They would be fun to play with.

Suddenly a light shone in Dunston's eyes. He looked up in surprise. The light came from a grate in the bathroom of the Grants' apartment. Curious, Dunston pressed his face to the grate. He was surprised to see someone stagger into the bathroom. Dunston smiled. This was the boy! The one who knew how to play with animals!

Dunston spied Kyle's old stuffed animal. What a nice dog! Quickly he shot an arm through the grate. He grabbed one of the dog's floppy ears and began to pull.

Half asleep, Kyle pulled back. "Cut it out," he muttered, yanking hard. The dog came free, and Kyle stumbled back to bed.

He was about to climb under the covers when his eyes popped open. He replayed what had just happened in his mind.

"Daaaaaaad!" he cried. "There's a monster in the bathroom!"

Kyle heard his father groan. In a moment Mr. Grant appeared at Kyle's door with his sleep mask pushed up on his forehead. "There's no monster, Kyle," Mr. Grant said. "You had a bad dream. That's all." He took Kyle's hand and led him out to the living room. He picked up the TV remote.

"Watch TV," Mr. Grant instructed. He clicked on the television. "There, an old black-and-white movie. That should put you to sleep." He handed Kyle the remote and wobbled back to his own bed.

Kyle sighed. How could he get his father to believe him? He stared at the TV, feeling frustrated. On the screen he saw a large gorilla. King

Kong! He looked something like the monster in the bathroom. But not exactly. The monster had reddish fur. . . .

This is *not* what I need to help me sleep! Kyle thought.

He turned off the television. There was a monster in the bathroom! Kyle was sure of it. The same monster he'd seen up on the roof!

Kyle thought hard. At last he came up with a plan.

Kyle hopped up from the couch. First he raided the refrigerator. He filled a bowl with lettuce, cereal, and bananas. He carried the bowl into the bathroom. Then he unscrewed the grate over the air-conditioning vent. He positioned the bowl right in front of the vent.

Finally he found the video camera. Kyle smiled, remembering how his mom used to record all their vacations. He took it into the bathroom and pointed it directly at the vent. Then he hid the camera under a pile of laundry. He made sure the lens wasn't covered. He pressed *record*.

Kyle smiled. In the morning he would have proof. He'd have his own monster movie!

CHAPTER 7

Late that night Dunston poked his head out of the vent. He sniffed the air. Bananas! Dunston climbed out into the bathroom. He reached for the bowl of food but stopped when he saw the blinking light of the video camera. Wow! thought Dunston. More shiny stuff!

Dunston brushed away the laundry and picked up the camera. He wondered if it was food. There was only one way to find out—he gave it a big lick. Yuck! It tasted awful. Dunston dropped the camera back onto the floor and reached for a banana. He didn't notice that the light had stopped flashing.

Dunston began to eat. He moved silently into the living room. Hey! There was the nice boy! He was sleeping on the couch. Dunston sat down beside Kyle while he finished the banana.

Kyle didn't wake up.

Dunston looked around the apartment. He liked it here. Maybe this would be a good place for a nest. Dunston decided to walk around. He ambled into Mr. Grant's room. There was someone in the big bed. It was a funny man! He wore a mask in bed! Dunston tapped him on the shoulder.

"Go to bed, Kyle." Mr. Grant groaned.

Dunston tapped him again.

"Okay," said Mr. Grant. "If you're still scared, you can sleep in here." He rolled over to make room. "Just for tonight."

What a nice invitation! This was even better than a nest! Dunston hopped into bed and snuggled up to Mr. Grant, giving him a little kiss.

"Thank you, Kyle," said Mr. Grant. "Now go to sleep."

Warm and comfortable, Dunston fell right to sleep.

The alarm sounded early the next morning. Mr. Grant turned it off while he was still half asleep.

Dunston jumped from the bed and slipped out of sight. He moved swiftly to the bathroom. There was that thing with the blinking light. He picked it up and hopped back into the vent.

Kyle opened one eye as his father came into the living room.

"Now you're on the couch, Kyle?" Mr. Grant asked. "Boy, you slept all over the place last night."

Kyle didn't know what his father meant. But he had more important things to think about.

"The bathroom!" he cried, leaping up from the couch. He zoomed toward the bathroom.

Mr. Grant chuckled. "He must really have to go," he said.

In the bathroom Kyle found a big mess. He grinned. The monster had trashed the place! And he had it all on film! His father would have to believe him now. Kyle reached under the laundry pile for the video camera.

It was gone.

After breakfast Kyle and Brian hurried down the hallway. Brian had a coiled rope slung over his shoulder.

"Wait till Dad finds out you lost the camera," Brian said.

"I didn't lose it," Kyle argued. "The monster did. I bet he tossed it down the laundry chute."

"Right," Brian said sarcastically. "The monster lost it."

"When we get it back, you'll see," said Kyle.

They passed a dark doorway. Neither Kyle nor Brian saw the man lurking in the shadows. It was Lord Rutledge. The boys didn't know that Rutledge had heard Kyle talking about a "monster." They didn't know that he began to follow them.

The boys took the service elevator to a closed-off area of the hotel. This hallway was being fixed up, so there were piles of new carpeting, paint

Meet the Grants! Kyle and his brother live in the
Majestic Hotel. Their dad is the hotel manager!

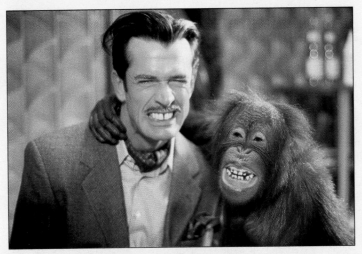

The Majestic has a secret guest. Nasty Lord
Rutledge has smuggled an orangutan named
Dunston into the hotel.

Lord Rutledge makes Dunston work in the hotel—
as a jewel thief.

Even though Dunston steals for Lord Rutledge, he
doesn't like being yelled at . . .

. . . so he gets mad! He decides to run away.

As he travels through the Majestic Hotel, Dunston meets Kyle!

Kyle promises to protect Dunston from Lord Rutledge. He tells Dunston to hide.

Dunston has fun hiding in a hotel room . . .

. . . until Lord Rutledge finds him. He's going to hurt Dunston with his terrifying pinchers.

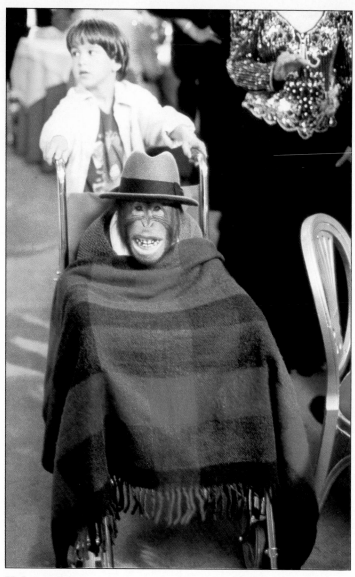

Kyle and Dunston escape into the ballroom—in disguise!

Meanwhile, Mr. Grant fights with Lord Rutledge in the hotel kitchen.

And Dunston hides until it's all over!

Now Dunston is part of the Grant family . . .

. . . until he has a family of his very own!

cans, wood, and construction tools everywhere. Brian put on his Rollerblade helmet. Kyle tied one end of the rope around his big brother's waist. Then he tied the other end to a pole across the hall.

Brian peered down the wide laundry chute. "Did I say I would do this for two months of your allowance, Kyle?" he asked.

Kyle nodded.

"Make it *three* months," Brian said.

Kyle tugged at the rope to make sure it was tied tightly.

Brian climbed over the edge of the chute. Kyle watched as he clicked on his flashlight and started down the tunnel.

Kyle let out the rope little by little. He was so busy concentrating on his brother that he never noticed the orangutan hiding behind the construction materials.

Kyle watched Brian move steadily down the chute, checking for evidence of the monster. Suddenly there was a loud clanging sound. A shaft of light fell on Brian's face. He froze.

Oh, no! It's a housekeeper! thought Kyle. She's opening the laundry chute upstairs. She'll catch Brian for sure!

But nobody looked into the chute. The housekeeper just tossed in a big pile of dirty linens. The laundry tumbled toward Brian, blocking Kyle's view. All Kyle saw were flying white sheets.

"Bri?" Kyle called softly down the chute. "You okay?"

"Yeah," Brian answered. "But now you owe me four months' allowance!" Kyle watched Brian untangle himself from bedsheets, towels, and pillowcases.

Kyle let the rope down some more. Dunston slipped out from his hiding place. He snuck up behind Kyle. Dunston happily popped a hotel mint into his mouth as he watched the nice boy play with the rope. It looked like fun!

"Found something!" Brian's voice floated up the laundry chute. "Some red hair got caught on a nail down here!"

Before Kyle could answer, the rope started jiggling.

"Hey!" cried Brian. "Kyle! What are you doing?"

Kyle stared at the rope. It bounced around in his hands, pulling him off-balance.

"Kyle!" Brian shouted from the chute. "What's going on?"

Kyle gulped. He didn't know what was going on! The rope danced around all by itself! There was only one explanation—the monster.

Taking a deep breath, Kyle whirled around. He forced himself to face the monster. But it wasn't a monster. Or even a gorilla. It was an orangutan! A real live orangutan in the Majestic Hotel!

Kyle was so surprised, he didn't even notice that Dunston was playing on the rope, swinging back and forth as though the rope were a jungle vine.

Brian yelled again. His voice wobbled as Dunston shook the rope, pulling it up and down. Brian's screams reminded Kyle that his brother was attached to the end of that rope! He took a few steps toward the orangutan.

"Could you . . . um, could you stop that? My brother's down there," he tried to explain. But the orangutan was putting on a show, swinging on the rope. Kyle cracked up. He couldn't help it!

"Kyle! I'm gonna kill you!" yelled Brian. Still laughing, Kyle gently took the orangutan's hands from the rope. He noticed that the orangutan had accidentally untied the rope from the pole. He tried to reach behind the friendly monster to tie it again, but Dunston grabbed Kyle's hand. Then he shook it up and down, as if they'd just been introduced.

Kyle smiled. He liked this monster.

"Dunston!" yelled a loud voice.

Startled, Kyle spun around. Lord Rutledge stood in front of him, waving a riding whip.

Yikes! Kyle was so frightened that he let go of the rope. It slid toward the chute. He dove for it, but he was too late. It slithered across the floor.

The end of the rope disappeared into the laundry chute!

"Kyyyylllle!" came Brian's voice, growing fainter as he fell. Kyle ran to the chute and peered down. He couldn't see his brother anywhere.

There was a sharp crack behind him. Kyle looked over his shoulder to see Lord Rutledge snapping his whip. Dunston squealed in fright.

"Hey! Leave him alone!" cried Kyle.

"You stay out of it!" Lord Rutledge growled at Kyle. Kyle noticed that Lord Rutledge's English accent was gone. That was weird, he thought.

"We have work to do, Dunston," said Lord Rutledge, moving in on the frightened orangutan.

"Hey!" Kyle yelled again. He charged at the mean man. At the same time Dunston leaned over and grabbed a piece of wood that lay on a bench. While Lord Rutledge pushed Kyle away, Dunston swung the board. Bam! It hit the nasty man!

Lord Rutledge doubled over in pain. Kyle watched in surprise as the orangutan scampered along the bench, jumped over Lord Rutledge, and launched himself into the air. Kyle's mouth dropped open. There was an orangutan flying right at him! Kyle backed up a step, but he hit the edge of the laundry chute. There was no place else to go!

Wham! Dunston hit Kyle with such force that

the two of them toppled into the laundry chute.

The boy and the orangutan screamed as they fell all the way down the chute. They hung on to each other on the way down. Finally they burst out of the chute and landed in a gigantic pile of dirty laundry!

Kyle couldn't see anything. He was buried in pillowcases. Then a long, reddish arm appeared. Dunston pulled Kyle out of the laundry pile.

"Okay . . . Dunston," said Kyle. "Let's get out of here before that nasty guy finds us."

Dunston took Kyle's hand as if he understood. He led the boy to the boiler room. It was dark there. Steam pipes hissed. Kyle had never liked that room—it was spooky. But Dunston showed Kyle a space behind one of the boilers. The orangutan had made a nest with sheets. In it were some fruit rinds. And the video camera! Videotape streamed from it.

"Dad's going to kill me," Kyle muttered.

Dunston grabbed the video camera and began wrapping the tape around it as if he were wrapping a present. He gave it to Kyle.

"Thanks." Kyle giggled.

Dunston smiled. He patted Kyle's face.

Kyle liked this orangutan. He wasn't anything like a monster. "Is that Rutledge guy always mean to you?" he asked softly.

Dunston looked sad when he heard that name.

"I bet he's not even a real lord!" Kyle said. He didn't care if Rutledge was mean to him. But nobody should be mean to an animal!

"Nobody's going to hurt you anymore," Kyle said, patting Dunston's head. "I promise."

CHAPTER 8

Kyle pushed a room-service cart down a hallway. A long white tablecloth covered the cart. No one seeing Kyle would have noticed anything suspicious. Not until he passed a dinner tray sitting in the hallway. Then a long, hairy arm darted out from under the cloth. The reddish hand grabbed the plate of leftovers off the tray. Dunston had snagged a snack!

Kyle kept his eye on the elevator at the end of the hall. If he could just get Dunston up to his apartment, his dad would tell him what to do. But the room-service cart was getting heavy. They passed the door marked MAJESTIC HOTEL SPA. Kyle whispered, "Almost there . . ."

Finally they reached the elevator. Kyle pressed the button. It took a long time for the elevator to arrive. Then Kyle heard the bell ring. The doors opened. And Rutledge stepped out!

Kyle gasped.

"Well, well . . . what have we here?" Rutledge sneered. He circled the covered cart. "Room service, hmmm?"

Under the tablecloth Dunston picked up Rutledge's scent. He wasn't going to let Rutledge find him. He wanted to stay with this nice boy!

As Rutledge circled, Dunston slipped out the opposite side of the cart. He scurried through the nearest door. He would hide until his boy found him.

Kyle saw Dunston escape out of the corner of his eye. The orangutan pushed through the door to the spa. Kyle didn't go after him—he knew an orangutan couldn't get into trouble in a health club! Instead he watched Rutledge.

The tall man squatted beside the cart. He yanked up the tablecloth. But Kyle knew Rutledge wouldn't find anything. With a frustrated yell Rutledge glanced around. The elevator doors were just closing. He lunged for the elevator, but the doors closed in his face. Rutledge let out another yell. He pounded on the doors with his fist.

Kyle smiled. Rutledge thought Dunston was in the elevator. Good! This would give him some time to find his friend.

As soon as the next elevator came, Rutledge stepped in. He gave Kyle a nasty look and said, "You and I must have a little . . . *talk* later."

Kyle didn't answer. He knew Rutledge didn't really want to talk. He wanted to make sure Kyle didn't tell anyone about Dunston. And about "Lord" Rutledge losing his English accent. But Kyle was *going* to tell someone—his dad! Just as soon as he found Dunston, that is.

The second the elevator doors closed, Kyle dashed into the spa. Where could Dunston be?

Dunston had wandered into the weight room. He found Mr. Spalding working out on a machine. The round man was pressing forty pounds of weights. He huffed and puffed as he struggled to lift the weights. His glasses were all steamed up. Dunston stood behind him, watching the weights go up and down.

This was a funny game!

Duston noticed something shiny. It was stuck under the weights as they moved up and down. Maybe it would taste good!

When Mr. Spalding paused to catch his breath, Dunston grabbed the metal rod that held up the weights. He gave it a big lick. Ugh! It tasted terrible! He dropped it on the floor. He went back to watching the man play with the weights.

But Dunston didn't know that he had taken out the pin that held the weights. Now there was no weight at all on the machine!

Mr. Spalding inhaled. He was pumping himself up for a big lift. With all his might, he pushed up. He expected the weights to be heavy. Instead they were really light. So light that Mr. Spalding went flying across the room! His thick glasses fell off and landed near Dunston's feet.

Glasses! Oh, boy! They were *really* shiny! Dunston picked them up. He put them on. Everything looked funny. Especially that round man crawling around on the floor. But the man looked angry. Dunston decided to leave. He spotted a door behind the weight machine and loped through it. Yahoo! He ran right into his boy!

"Come on!" Kyle said, grabbing Dunston's hand. "Let's go!"

They started out of the men's locker room. Then Kyle spotted Rutledge. He was questioning the woman at the spa desk. Kyle quickly pulled Dunston into another small room.

Inside it two women seemed to be sleeping. Their faces were covered in green goo. Their heads were wrapped in towels. One woman had cucumber slices over her eyes.

"Stay here," Kyle whispered to Dunston. Then Kyle went to spy on Rutledge.

Dunston walked over to the woman with the cucumbers on her eyes. The green stuff on her face looked tasty. He licked it. It was good! He licked some more. Then he plucked off the cucumber slices and popped them into his mouth. Delicious!

He scooted out the door before the woman opened her eyes.

Meanwhile Kyle had been trying to find a way

out of the spa—a way that didn't go past the reception desk. He couldn't find one. As he stuck his head out into the hallway, he saw his father and Brian running toward the spa.

"There he is!" Brian yelled, pointing at Kyle. "He dropped me down the laundry chute!"

Kyle ignored his brother. "Dad!" he cried. "There isn't a monster in the hotel!"

"I know that, Kyle," said his father.

"There's an *orangutan* in the hotel," Kyle explained. He took his father's hand and began dragging him toward the room where he had left Dunston. "His name is Dunston. And that English guy is really mean to him."

Mr. Grant stopped walking. "You don't mean Lord Rutledge, do you?" he asked.

"He's not really a lord," Kyle said. "His accent is phony!"

"Kyle," said his father. "Lord Rutledge is here to rate the Majestic Hotel! It's very important that we treat him well. Mrs. Dubrow will be angry if Lord Rutledge doesn't like it here."

"But *Dad!*" cried Kyle. "Look!" He flung open the door of the little room.

The two women with green goo on their faces screamed.

"Sorry, ladies," said Mr. Grant, closing the door.

He pulled Kyle into the hall. "What is the matter with you? This is not what I need. The

Crystal Ball is tomorrow!"

"I see why this hotel is run so badly," said a voice with an English accent. Kyle glanced up. Lord Rutledge!

"You can't even control one small boy," he continued.

"You're in trouble now!" Kyle yelled at him. "My dad's here!"

Mr. Grant reached out and pulled Kyle toward him. "I'm terribly, terribly sorry, Lord Rutledge," he said.

Shocked, Kyle stared up at his dad. Why was he being nice? Kyle had just told him Rutledge was a phony!

"He's very sorry," repeated Mr. Grant. "Aren't you, Kyle?"

"No!" cried Kyle. "He tried to hurt Dunston!"

"Your son is a lunatic," declared Lord Rutledge.

"Apologize, Kyle," Mr. Grant commanded. "Now."

"Sorry," he mumbled. Then he turned and ran down the hall.

Kyle felt like crying. Why didn't his dad believe him? Was some dumb hotel rating more important than he was?

CHAPTER 9

Dunston peeked around the spa door. There was his boy! He had another boy with him. And a man! This man looked nicer than Rutledge. Dunston started toward them.

But there was Rutledge! Now he was talking to the nice man. Dunston scooted down the hall. He wasn't going to get caught again. Maybe he could see his boy later. Near the hotel kitchen, Dunston made his way back into the air-conditioning system. But not before he found some snacks!

Dunston sat in the air-conditioning duct, thinking and eating. Maybe he'd go to his nest. But it was so dark down there. Dark and sort of scary. Dunston decided to see what was at the top of the hotel. He began climbing up the vent.

This was a tall hotel! At last Dunston came to a grate. He saw sunlight. And best of all, he spied a tree! Dunston stuck his arm through the grate. He reached as far as he could . . . and grabbed a leaf. Then he pulled his arm back in and took a nibble. Yum! This was even better than room-service food! It was almost as good as a banana!

Dunston pushed with all his might. The grate popped off! When Dunston climbed out of the vent, he found himself in a greenhouse jungle. He was home!

Dunston picked one leaf after another. Delicious! Finally he had eaten enough. He looked around the greenhouse. Maybe he could find a nice place to curl up for a nap. But then he looked out the greenhouse window.

It was the nice man! The one who knew his boy! He was playing with a lot of papers. That looked like fun.

Dunston skipped over to the window. He pressed his face flat against the glass. He knew it made his face look so funny! Now all he had to do was wait until the nice man looked up.

There! The nice man looked! But why wasn't he laughing? Why was he yelling? Why was he leaping up and down?

Oh, well. Dunston sighed as he stepped away from the glass. He spotted a pretty tree. Dunston sprang up and grabbed one of its branches. He began happily swinging back and forth. Then he climbed up into the tree. The orangutan sat on a fat branch and gazed around. It was good to be home.

On the other side of the greenhouse glass Mr. Grant had been having a meeting. But now he was yelling into the phone. There was a monkey in the Majestic Hotel! A monkey in the rooftop greenhouse!

Mr. Grant called down to his office. His assistant, Nancy, answered the phone. "Send security up to the roof," he told Nancy. "And call an animal-control person. There's a monkey in my hotel!"

Mr. Grant slammed down the phone. Then he picked it up again. He called Nancy back. "And call Kyle and apologize for me," he said. "I should have believed him."

Mr. Grant gazed through the glass. He couldn't see the monkey anymore. But he had to find him—a monkey could really ruin the Crystal Ball! And what if Lord Rutledge saw a monkey running around the five-star hotel? He would go back to the hotel-rating people and tell them the Majestic Hotel was a zoo!

He had to find the monkey.

Several minutes later Dunston heard someone calling, "Monkey? Where are you, monkey?"

Dunston yawned. He had been dreaming about Samson. But it sounded like there was a man in his jungle. Dunston pushed away the leaves in front of his face and looked down.

It was the nice man! Maybe he wanted to play! Dunston leaped down from his branch. He bounded over to Mr. Grant and gave him a great big hug.

The nice man screeched. So Dunston screeched back.

Wow! The nice man sure squirmed around a lot. And he made such funny hooting sounds! Dunston hung on. What a wild hug!

Kyle lay on his bed and stared at the ceiling. How could he make his dad believe him? He knew Rutledge was a big phony. He knew there was an orangutan in the hotel. But how could he prove it to his father?

The phone rang. Kyle padded out into the living room to answer it.

"Hello?"

It was Nancy. Kyle listened for a moment. "Dad saw Dunston?" he exclaimed. "In the greenhouse? That's great!" Kyle listened again. "But . . . he couldn't have attacked Dad!" he declared. "No! He'd never do that. He's really gentle!"

Kyle couldn't understand what else Nancy was saying. Something about an animal-control expert? He hung up and dashed out of the apartment. He took the elevator down to the lobby and zoomed straight to his father's office.

"Dad!" Kyle cried as he burst through the office door. He stopped short. In front of him stood Mrs. Dubrow. And a man wearing a safari suit. And waving a rifle!

"Hey!" Kyle shouted. "What's he doing with that gun?"

"Mr. LaFarge is just showing it to us, Kyle," his father explained. Mr. Grant put his arm around Kyle's shoulders and herded him toward the door. "Sorry I didn't believe you about the monkey," he whispered.

"He's an orangutan," Kyle corrected his dad.

"The orangutan, then," Mr. Grant said. "Take off now, okay?"

"Okay," Kyle agreed. His father closed the door, but Kyle put his ear to the crack and listened. He wanted to know why that safari man had a gun.

"This is a tranquilizer gun," Mr. LaFarge was saying. "One dart will knock out a human for eighteen hours."

"What will it do to an orangutan?" Mrs. Dubrow asked.

"Kill him, most likely," said Mr. LaFarge.

Kyle's eyes grew wide as he listened.

"Why?" Mr. LaFarge asked. "Do you want him alive?"

"No," said Mrs. Dubrow.

Kyle didn't wait to hear anymore. He took off, heading for the greenhouse. He had to find Dunston before Mr. LaFarge did! He took a service elevator straight to the top floor of the Majestic Hotel. But he was too late!

Murray and the security guards were just about to enter the greenhouse. Kyle knew he had to head them off. To keep them away from Dunston. He thought fast.

"Murray!" he called to the security chief. "The monkey's down in the kitchen! You'd better get down there. Dad's pretty mad!"

"Thanks, kid!" said Murray. "Okay, guys! Let's go!"

They all got on the elevator. Kyle waited until they were gone. Then he stepped into the greenhouse.

"Dunston?" he called softly. "It's me!"

Dunston peeked out from behind a clump of bushes.

"Dunston!" exclaimed Kyle, grinning.

The orangutan jumped with joy as Kyle rushed over to him. Kyle grabbed Dunston's hand.

"Come on, boy," he said. "We have to get you out of here."

Just then Mr. LaFarge kicked open the greenhouse door. He stomped in, his tranquilizer gun ready.

They were trapped!

Kyle dove under a bush, pulling Dunston with him. He put an arm around the trembling animal. "I won't let them hurt you," he promised.

Mr. LaFarge began poking the barrel of his gun into nearby bushes. Kyle held his breath. Maybe if they were very quiet, he wouldn't find them. He glanced at Dunston. Oh, no! Dunston thought Mr. LaFarge was playing a game! The dart gun poked in again and Dunston grabbed it. He hung from the barrel as if it were a tree branch!

Mr. LaFarge gasped. He tried to shake the animal off his gun. But Dunston held tight. Then he stuck out his tongue.

Kyle's mind was spinning. Dunston didn't know that he was swinging from a gun! He didn't realize this safari man wanted to hurt him!

Kyle had an idea. He stooped down. Quickly he tied Mr. LaFarge's bootlaces together in a knot. The hunter was too busy yelling at Dunston to notice. Kyle made the biggest knot he could. He'd barely finished when Dunston got bored with his game and swung off the gun barrel. He leaped up into a tree. Mr. LaFarge raised his rifle.

He aimed.

He tried to steady himself by taking a step forward and—plop! He fell on his face. The gun went off, blasting a huge hole in the greenhouse glass.

Kyle stayed in his hiding place. He watched Dunston escape through the hole in the broken window. Go, boy! he thought.

As Dunston disappeared, Mrs. Dubrow burst in. "Did you get him?" she asked Mr. LaFarge.

"Um . . . not yet," said Mr. LaFarge.

Kyle peeked out from the bushes. He saw that Mr. LaFarge was staring down at the knot in his shoelaces.

"I have a strong feeling," Mr. LaFarge added, "that we're dealing with a *very* smart animal here."

CHAPTER 10

"Dad? That Rutledge guy—" Kyle began. He was tagging after his father. Mr. Grant paced back and forth on the balcony overlooking the lobby of the Majestic Hotel.

"Kyle," his father interrupted. "I admit I was wrong about the monk—uh, the orangutan. But Lord Rutledge is an important guest—the *most* important guest. If he's not happy here, I could get fired. So you be nice to him."

Mr. Grant held a cellular phone to his ear. Now he said into it, "Murray? Find Mr. LaFarge. Take away his gun. I don't want a nut with a loaded weapon running through my hotel. Especially not right before the Crystal Ball!"

"But Rutledge—" Kyle said again.

"*Lord* Rutledge has nothing to do with the monkey," Mr. Grant insisted. "Mrs. Dubrow says he's here to rate the hotel. He could give us a sixth star!"

Kyle made a face. Who cared about a stupid star? He only cared about Dunston.

A yapping sound from the lobby made Kyle look down. Mr. LaFarge stalked through the lobby with a large bloodhound on a leash. The blood-hound sniffed the marble floor. He was hot on the trail of . . . Mr. Spalding's little dog, Neil!

"Murray? I've found Mr. LaFarge," Mr. Grant said into the phone. "I'm going down to the lobby now."

Kyle gave up. His father would never believe Rutledge was a phony. Kyle had to find Dunston himself. Somehow he had to hide Dunston from Rutledge—*and* from Mr. LaFarge!

He hurried down to the boiler room, hoping Dunston would be in his nest. Kyle felt so worried that he wasn't even afraid of the spooky boiler room. He just hoped Dunston was there!

He made his way through the maze of steamy pipes. As he got close to Dunston's nest, he noticed something on the floor.

Kyle gasped. It looked like blood!

"Dunston?" he called. "Are you here? It's me!"

Dunston peeked out from behind the furnace. He gave Kyle a weak smile. Then he held out his arm. It was bleeding! A small piece of green glass stuck out from the cut.

"Poor Dunston," Kyle said soothingly. "You cut yourself on the greenhouse. I'll fix you up."

Cautiously Kyle led Dunston to his apartment.

"Brian?" Kyle called, pushing open the front door. "Brian! We need help!"

Brian looked up from his computer. He stared

at his brother and the orangutan. Dunston waved.

"Holy cow!" Brian exclaimed.

The boys took Dunston into Kyle's room. Brian pulled out the first-aid kit and found some tweezers. He tried to remove the sliver of glass from the orangutan's arm. But Dunston kept flinching.

"Hold him, Kyle!" Brian said.

"It's hard," Kyle explained. "He's scared."

"Do what Dad does," Brian suggested. "Sing to him."

Kyle didn't know if it would work, but he started singing. Dunston clapped his hands over his ears. But he didn't smile.

"I know it hurts, Dunston," Kyle said. "But it's for your own good. Just look at me."

The orangutan stared into Kyle's eyes.

"That's right," Kyle whispered. "It's gonna be okay."

"Got it!" Brian cried. He held up the glass in the tweezers.

Kyle washed the wound and bandaged it. Then the boys sat with Dunston on Kyle's bed.

"If we can hide him for a couple of days—" Kyle began.

"Then what?" asked Brian. "Get him a job in the kitchen?"

"There's the zoo," Kyle suggested. "At least nobody would be mean to him. And he'd have other monkeys to hang with." Kyle frowned, thinking. "We can hide him in my room."

"Dad's pretty crazed with the Crystal Ball coming up and all," Brian said. "But I think he'd notice an orangutan in your room."

Both boys stared at the wall, deep in thought. Suddenly Brian's face lit up. "Hey! Wait a minute. We've got *lots* of rooms."

Brian bolted over to his computer. He called up the Majestic Hotel guest register. "What name would he like?" Brian asked.

Kyle opened a phone book in front of Dunston. Dunston covered his eyes with one hand. With the other he pointed to a name in the book.

Kyle squinted down at the phone book. "Lam Binh Ngoc," he managed at last.

"Let's make him *Dr*. Lam Binh Ngoc," Brian suggested. "If the hotel thinks you're a doctor, you can get away with anything." He entered the information.

Ten minutes later Kyle and Brian pushed a hotel wheelchair down a hallway. In the chair sat Dunston. He wore a hat, glasses, and an overcoat. With a blanket wrapped around his shoulders, he looked like a small, hairy old man.

"Uh-oh," whispered Brian. "Here comes Artie."

Kyle saw the old bellman coming toward them down the hallway. But as usual Artie was staring at the floor. He didn't even glance at the boys.

"Whew!" said Brian. He pulled out a passkey. "That was a close one." He opened the door to the Majestic's presidential suite. The boys surveyed the enormous rooms in awe. Dunston happily hopped out of his chair and began exploring.

"You think this fancy suite is a good idea?" asked Kyle.

"The more respectable you seem, the less people hassle you," declared Brian. "Why do you think I dress nice?"

Soon they all felt at home in the suite. Dunston and Kyle banged out a duet on the baby-grand piano. Brian picked up the phone. "Room service?" he said in a fake deep voice. "I'd like two banana splits with extra bananas. One fruit salad—no, make that two. Extra bananas in each."

As he hung up, his beeper went off. "Uh-oh. It's Dad," he said. "We're late for our dinner. Come on."

"What about room service?" asked Kyle.

"If nobody answers, they come back," said Brian knowingly.

Kyle hesitated.

"Trust me," said Brian. "I've got it all figured out."

Kyle glanced back at Dunston. "Be good!" he told him.

Dunston nodded innocently.

Alone in the room, Dunston opened the mini-bar. The gold foil on the top of a bottle of sparkling apple cider caught his eye. Shiny stuff! He pulled out the bottle and tore off the foil. *Pop!* A cork flew out of the bottle! It sailed across the room.

Dunston screeched. He dropped the bottle and scampered to the other side of the room.

Cautiously he peered around. The bottle lay on its side, gushing cider. It didn't make any more loud noises. Dunston approached it warily. He stuck a finger in the liquid and tasted it. Yum!

Next Dunston took a nice warm bubble bath. He sipped the cider while he watched TV from the tub. Suddenly he sat up straight. Someone was knocking at the door! Had his boys come back?

Dunston leaped from the tub. He threw on a Majestic Hotel bathrobe and galloped out to answer the door.

"Evening, Dr. Ngoc," said Artie, his eyes on the floor. He wheeled a room-service cart into the room. "Where would you like this?"

Dunston hopped up on a chair and hooted.

"Sorry, doctor," Artie continued, still not looking up. "I don't speak your language. Over here all right?"

Dunston hooted again.

"Fine," said Artie. Then he handed Dunston the bill and a pen. He went over to set things up on the table.

Dunston scribbled on the bill. Then he handed it back.

"Thank you, Dr. Ngoc," Artie said. "Good night."

Dunston warbled pleasantly as Artie left. Then he perched on the arm of his chair, spread his napkin on his knee, and dug in!

Kyle and Brian came back to the presidential suite after dinner. They surveyed the mess with amazement.

"They actually gave room service to a monkey!" exclaimed Brian, shaking his head.

"Come on, Dunston," said Kyle. "Play time!"

Kyle threw every pillow in the suite into a pile on the floor. Then they played a wild game of Frisbee. First Kyle hit the pillows as he made his catch. Then he tossed the Frisbee to Brian. Brian tossed it to Dunston, who caught it with his feet!

"All right, Dunston!" cried Brian and Kyle.

After a while they were all worn out. Dunston made himself a nest with blankets and pillows on top of the dresser.

"Let's go," Brian said. "We don't want Dad looking for us."

Kyle reached up and patted Dunston's head.

83

"Don't worry," Kyle reassured him. "We'll be back tomorrow. And we'll get you out of here to a place where you'll be safe. I promise." Dunston pulled Kyle close and gave him a big, wet kiss.

The boys dimmed the lights and left the presidential suite. Brian hung a Do Not Disturb sign on the doorknob.

"Thanks, Bri," Kyle said as they headed for the elevator.

Brian put an arm around his little brother. "I'm grounded anyway," he teased. "I have to do *something*."

CHAPTER 11

"Everybody's getting ready for that stupid Crystal Ball," Kyle told Dunston the next evening. He was dressing the orangutan in his little old man outfit again. "It's about to start. I can sneak you out the back way." He put on the hat. "Nobody will notice. They're all too busy."

Kyle stepped back and looked at Dunston sadly. "I have to take you to the zoo," he said. "It's not that great. But at least they'll be nice to you. And I can visit you every day."

A knock sounded at the door.

Kyle grinned. "Brian's here!" To Dunston he added, "I'm not supposed to cross the street by myself."

Kyle ran for the door. But before he got there, it swung open. There stood Rutledge, dressed in a tuxedo. He held up a metal stick. He had picked the lock!

"You again." Rutledge sneered.

Kyle's heart sank. "How did you find us?" he asked.

"It wasn't too hard," Rutledge said. "I simply hooked up my computer to the hotel's database and did a word search. And guess which word I chose?"

Kyle shrugged.

Rutledge gave a cold smile. "Banana!" he said gleefully. "'Dr. Ngoc' in the presidential suite must really like bananas. Right, Dunston?"

Once more Kyle pushed "old man" Dunston in the wheelchair. But this time Rutledge was by his side. He made sure they went to his hotel room. When they were inside, Rutledge dragged Kyle into the bathroom and tied him up. He covered Kyle's mouth with masking tape. Then he filled the bathtub with pillows and shoved Kyle into the tub. Kyle couldn't move. And he was so terrified that he could hardly breathe!

"That'll take care of you," Rutledge growled. "Now say good-bye to Dunston. He's just become a *really* endangered species."

Kyle's eyes widened in fright as the meaning of Rutledge's words sank in. He was going to kill Dunston!

Rutledge stomped out of the bathroom. Through the open door Kyle saw Rutledge move toward Dunston. "Give me those jewels!" he yelled, pointing at Dunston's fanny pack. "And then get to work while I'm at the Crystal Ball!"

Kyle saw Dunston open his arms wide in a friendly gesture.

"Yes," hissed Rutledge. "Give Daddy a hug. And after you do one last job, you'll be joining your brother—forever."

Kyle frowned. What had Rutledge done to Dunston's brother?

Kyle watched Dunston throw his arms around Rutledge. And then Dunston opened his mouth and bit the tall man's ear.

"Yeooow!" Rutledge screamed. He dropped the orangutan. Dunston dashed in the direction of the door.

"Noooo!" cried Rutledge. "Get back here with those jewels!" He ran out of the room after Dunston.

Kyle listened as Rutledge's footsteps grew faint. He guessed that Dunston had escaped. Yes!

Dunston hadn't gone far. He was crouched on a radiator pipe above the hotel-room door. He waited until Rutledge was out of sight. Then he swung back into the room. He trotted right to the bathroom.

Kyle was thrilled to see his friend. Dunston grabbed the end of the masking tape across Kyle's mouth. In one swift move he yanked it off.

Ouch!

Kyle put his hand to his mouth and screamed.

Dunston hooted and pointed at Kyle.

"Thanks, Dunston," Kyle said after Dunston

untied him. "Let's get out of here."

As he passed Dunston's trunk, Kyle spotted the photograph of O'Malley's orangutans. Dunston stuck out a finger. He patted the picture of Samson.

"So this is you and your brother," Kyle said. "And Mr. O'Malley! I knew he wasn't Lord Rutledge!" Dunston pointed to the picture. Then he unzipped his fanny pack. Kyle looked inside. "Mrs. Dellacroce's jewelry!" he cried. "Rutledge isn't just a phony," he realized. "He's a jewel thief!"

Kyle tore the newspaper clipping off Dunston's trunk. Finally he had proof that Rutledge was a phony! He stuck the paper into his pocket. Then he led Dunston over to a panel in the wall. He slid it back, revealing a small, rickety platform.

"It's called a dumbwaiter," Kyle explained to Dunston. "It's like a little elevator—they used to send dishes back to the kitchen on this thing. Come on!" He and Dunston climbed aboard the small platform inside the dumbwaiter. Kyle closed the door behind them.

"Don't be scared," Kyle told Dunston as he began lowering the platform. "My dad's going to help us."

Down, down they went. With a bump they landed on the lobby floor of the hotel. Kyle opened the door and stuck out his head. He could hear people laughing and glasses clinking. The famous Crystal Ball had begun. Kyle motioned to Dunston to get out of the dumbwaiter. Quietly he led him down a service hallway to the storage room.

Dunston sat in a wheelchair. He was dressed in his little old man clothes again. And he smiled and waved at everybody as Kyle pushed him— into the ballroom!

Kyle took a deep breath. He had to find his dad, and he wasn't going to risk leaving Dunston again. But the ballroom was huge! Hundreds of people in tuxedos and sparkling dresses filled the room. Where was his dad? Kyle searched the room.

He saw Mr. LaFarge, wearing a purple tuxedo. A lump in his jacket showed Kyle where his tranquilizer gun was. Yikes!

Next he noticed Mr. Spalding. Kyle had never seen him without his dog before.

Then he spotted Rutledge! Kyle saw the tall man's eyes go wide as he caught sight of Kyle and Dunston. But before Rutledge could grab him, someone grabbed Rutledge!

"Lord Rutledge," cooed Mrs. Dubrow. "It's very important to me that you enjoy yourself at the Majestic. I want you to be my special guest for the ball."

Mrs. Dubrow pulled Rutledge away. He

glanced back at Kyle and scowled.

"That was close!" Kyle whispered. He turned to Dunston. But the wheelchair was empty. Dunston was gone!

Oh, no, thought Kyle. Dunston must have gotten scared when he saw Rutledge! The orangutan must be hiding somewhere in the ballroom. But Kyle saw Rutledge looking around. And Mr. LaFarge was searching for Dunston too!

I have to find Dad, thought Kyle. He glanced around the room and spotted Brian. He was standing in a corner of the lobby, watching the ball. Kyle ran over to him. "Where's Dad?" he asked.

"Somewhere in here," answered Brian. "What's up?"

Kyle handed his brother the O'Malley's orangutans photo. Brian looked at it and then took off running. Kyle took off after him.

They ran up to Mr. Grant, who was chatting with a guest.

"Excuse me a moment," Mr. Grant said to the guest. He turned toward his sons. "What are you two doing here?" he demanded.

"Dad, take a look at this," said Brian.

Kyle held out the photo of Rutledge and the orangutans.

Mr. Grant scanned it while his sons filled him in on what had been happening.

"Rutledge tied you up?" he asked Kyle.

Kyle nodded. "He's the one who stole Mrs. Dellacroce's jewels," he said. "And I don't know what he'll do to Dunston if he finds him!"

"You two find the monkey," said Mr. Grant, storming off toward the buffet table. "I'll take care of 'Lord' Rutledge."

Kyle and Brian exchanged glances. They'd never seen their dad so worked up.

"Come on," said Kyle. "I know Dunston is in here somewhere."

Dunston was bored. He'd been hiding under the table in the ballroom ever since he saw Rutledge. Where was his boy? he wondered. He couldn't smell him anywhere. Dunston decided to look around.

He snuck over to the next table and crawled under the tablecloth. He saw legs! A man and a woman sat at the table. Dunston couldn't see their faces. He didn't know the man was Mr. Spalding.

Dunston stared at the woman's dress. It was covered in shiny stuff! Gold spangles! Those spangles were so nice. Dunston tried to pluck one off.

"Stop that!" cried the woman.

Dunston stopped. He peeked out at the table. There was a glass. Come to think of it, he was thirsty. Dunston reached out a large hairy hand

and grabbed the glass. He brought it under the table. Yum! This tasted good. Maybe there was something else tasty up there. Swiftly Dunston stuck his hand up again. He felt around on the table. There! He found a snack on a toothpick.

Dunston popped the food into his mouth. Mmmm!

Just then someone lifted up the tablecloth. Dunston froze. But it wasn't Rutledge. It was the man he'd seen in the spa! The man with the shiny glasses! Dunston grinned at him. To show that he liked the man, Dunston rested his head in his lap.

"Aheeee!" cried Mr. Spalding. "There's a monkey in my lap!"

Quickly Dunston sat straight up. Why was the man with glasses making such a fuss? Now he had to get out of here. Dunston darted out from under Mr. Spalding's table. He sniffed the air. Rutledge! Dunston smelled Rutledge! He was trapped!

"I've got you now," muttered Rutledge. He threw a big tablecloth over Dunston's head. Then he tied up Dunston like a bundle of laundry. He swung the tablecloth over his shoulder and took off for the kitchen.

What a bumpy ride! Dunston didn't like it one bit.

"There you are!" someone shouted. It was the nice man's voice! The nice man he had hugged in the jungle! Maybe the nice man would help him get away from Rutledge.

"You tied up my kid!" yelled the nice man's voice.

Dunston peeked out through a gap in the tablecloth. He saw a shiny silver counter. Hey! Dunston knew this place. It was the kitchen, where they kept lots of snacks!

Dunston watched Rutledge grab a big knife. Then he held it up, ready to throw it. "I learned a lot of useful things in the circus," Rutledge said.

"What happened to your British accent?" asked the nice man.

"You have exactly three seconds to get out of my way!" Rutledge replied. He began counting. "One . . ."

Dunston didn't want the nice man to get hurt. He wriggled his arm into the gap in the table-cloth. He reached out. His hand felt a heavy frying pan. He grasped it by the handle.

"Two . . ." counted Rutledge.

Dunston slowly drew the frying pan up and back.

"Three!" cried Rutledge. As he stepped for-ward to throw the knife, Dunston slammed the pan down on his head.

BOIIINNNG!

Dunston heard the knife clatter to the floor as Rutledge lost his grip on the weapon—and on the tablecloth. Quickly he struggled free.

"Monkey!" cried Mr. Grant. "Go! Get out of here!"

Dunston leaped up, grabbing a lamp that hung from the ceiling. Away he swung, high above the kitchen tables. In no time Dunston reached the door. He glanced back. Rutledge and the nice man were dueling, trying to hit each other with frying pans.

Dunston swung out to the ballroom. He'd had enough of hiding under tables. Now he began to climb up a tall column. He climbed all the way to the ceiling. He leaped from the column to the ballroom's huge crystal chandelier. It swung gently as he landed. He gazed down. Below, hundreds of men and women were dancing.

This is a nice place to sit! thought Dunston. He plucked off a crystal from the chandelier. It was really shiny! He licked it. But it tasted yucky! Dunston let the crystal drop. He watched as it fell down, down, down. *Plop!* It landed right in a woman's drink!

The startled woman looked up to see where it had come from.

Dunston grinned at her and waved.

Dunston hoped she would wave back. But she didn't.

"A monkey!" she screamed, pointing to the chandelier. "A monkey in the Majestic Hotel!"

94

CHAPTER 12

Kyle grinned. At last he had found Dunston. He watched the orangutan swing back and forth on the chandelier. Dunston was safe up there, he thought. At least for the moment.

Kyle's thoughts were interrupted by Mrs. Dubrow's voice. She screamed at Mr. LaFarge.

"Shoot that beast!" she cried. "Shoot him!"

Mr. LaFarge pulled the tranquilizer gun from under his jacket. He took aim at Dunston.

"No!" shouted Kyle. He raced toward Mr. LaFarge. "Don't shoot!"

But Kyle was too late. Mr. LaFarge pulled the trigger. The gunfire sent the Crystal Ball guests stampeding for the exits.

Horrified, Kyle stared up at the chandelier. He saw that the dart had shattered some crystals. But it had missed Dunston. He let out a sigh of relief.

Kyle looked back at Mr. LaFarge. He was aiming for a second shot! Mrs. Dubrow stood by him, urging him to hurry.

Kyle ran for them. He broke through the crowd and grabbed Mr. LaFarge's arm just as he

95

pulled the trigger. The gun fired low, into the crowd. Mr. Spalding jumped in pain. Quickly he reached around and yanked a dart out of the back of his leg.

As a crowd gathered around Mr. Spalding, Kyle grabbed Mr. LaFarge's dart gun. He slid it under a buffet table where Chef Bernard had just put out a beautiful five-layer cake. Then Kyle ran over to Brian.

"Where's Dad?" he asked, panting.

"He's coming," said Brian. "Look!"

Kyle glanced at the kitchen door. All of a sudden Rutledge came flying through the door. He fell on the floor, out cold.

"Wow!" whispered Kyle.

He looked up just in time to see his dad barge through the door. He held a frying pan in his hand. Kyle thought he looked just like Arnold Schwarzenegger.

"That was for tying up my kid!" Mr. Grant yelled, shaking the frying pan at Rutledge.

"Cool!" cried Kyle. He checked the chandelier. There was Dunston. Safe and sound. He waved up at the orangutan.

Suddenly Mrs. Dubrow's hand clamped down on his shoulder.

"You did this!" she shrieked at Kyle. She started shaking him. "You brought that monkey into my hotel!"

                              * * *

Dunston looked down from above. He saw his
boy! That woman was hurting him!

"You little brat!" screamed Mrs. Dubrow.

Dunston frowned. No one was allowed to hurt
his nice boy!

Dunston moved to the edge of the shiny chandelier. He got ready to jump.

Kyle braced himself. He knew Mrs. Dubrow
was going to slap him. But all of a sudden she
froze. Kyle glanced up. He saw why. Dunston was
charging full speed ahead at Mrs. Dubrow!

Before she could scream, Dunston smashed
into her. She staggered forward, landing face-
down in Chef Bernard's cake.

"All right, Dunston!" cried Kyle.

But Dunston wasn't finished yet. Mrs. Dubrow
struggled out of the cake and Dunston jumped on
her again. He began licking the frosting from her
face.

"Victor!" Mrs. Dubrow screamed. "Help me!"

But Kyle saw that Mr. Dubrow was doubled
over. He was laughing his head off!

Mrs. Dubrow was furious. Kyle saw her looking around the room for someone to help her. Her
eyes fell on Mr. LaFarge's dart gun on the floor.
Oh, no!

She lunged for it.

Kyle let out a loud scream.

And Mr. Grant's hands came down on Mrs. Dubrow's shoulders. "Don't even think about it," Mr. Grant said as he let her go. She tumbled off her six-inch heels and back into the cake.

"You're fired!" Mrs. Dubrow screamed at Mr. Grant. "You'll never work in a hotel again!"

Mr. Grant shrugged.

"All right, Dad!" cried Kyle.

Mrs. Dubrow furiously wiped icing from her hair. She stopped when she noticed Mr. Spalding. He held out the tranquilizer dart that had hit him in the leg.

"Mrs. Dubrow," he said woozily. "My name is Lionel Spalding. I'm with the hotel-rating organization."

"You?" Mrs. Dubrow's mouth dropped open.

"Congratulations, Mrs. Dubrow," Mr. Spalding continued.

Kyle saw Mrs. Dubrow smile hopefully.

"You have gone from a five-star hotel . . ." Mr. Spalding began.

Mrs. Dubrow's smile broadened.

" . . . to a *one*-star hotel. Good night."

Mr. Spalding fainted as the tranquilizer began working. He toppled into Mrs. Dubrow, knocking her back into the cake.

Mr. Dubrow exploded with laughter all over again.

* * *

Kyle sat with Dunston and Brian as the police questioned Rutledge. Kyle had given them Dunston's fanny pack, filled with Mrs. Dellacroce's stolen jewelry. The police put Rutledge in handcuffs and led him away.

He scowled at Dunston as he passed.

Dunston stuck out his tongue.

Mr. LaFarge followed the police. But he stopped in front of Dunston and held out his hand. "I was just doing my job," he told the orangutan. "It was nothing personal."

Dunston looked at Kyle. Kyle nodded.

And Dunston belted Mr. LaFarge right on the jaw!

Mr. LaFarge fell to the ground. As he lay there he said, "I deserved that."

Kyle's dad came over to sit with them. "In my entire life, I've never struck another human being," he told his sons.

"You were so cool, Dad," said Kyle. "You really were."

Brian looked thoughtful. "But you do realize that by tonight, we'll probably be living in a motel on a highway somewhere."

Mr. Grant just sighed. Then he turned to Kyle. "I'm sorry I didn't believe you." He leaned over and hugged his son.

Kyle hugged back. Then Dunston draped one

long arm over the two of them. With the other he reached out and pulled Brian into a big group hug.

CHAPTER 13

The next morning there was a knock at the door. The Grants were busy packing up their apartment. Kyle knew Dunston would have to go to the zoo that afternoon. This was probably the humane-society people, coming to take him away.

Kyle turned to Dunston. "It's a really nice zoo," he said. "And you'll have friends."

Dunston patted Kyle's head.

"No, I mean monkey friends," Kyle said. "And I don't know where we'll be, but I'll try to come visit you . . ."

There was another knock. A loud knock.

Dragging his feet, Kyle went to answer the door. There stood Mr. Dubrow.

"Morning, Kyle," he said. He stepped into the apartment.

"Where's Mrs. Dubrow?" Kyle asked suspiciously.

"Scouting hotel sites in Alaska," Mr. Dubrow said. "It's probably going to take her a *long* time. But what I came to say is, Robert, I want you to stay."

Shocked, Kyle stared at his father. Brian grinned.

"I'm very flattered," said Mr. Grant. "But no thanks."

Brian groaned. Kyle smiled. He didn't want to stay in this boring hotel. Not without Dunston.

"This is the finest hotel in my chain," said Mr. Dubrow.

"I know," said Mr. Grant. "But, well, I'd like a position that's . . ." He glanced at Kyle and Brian. "Not quite so demanding on my time."

Mr. Dubrow looked thoughtful. "Let me see what I can do."

About a year later Kyle stood with his brother and his father in the courtyard of their new hotel. The tropical sun was bright up above, glinting off the clear blue water that surrounded the Bali Majestic Hotel.

Kyle's dad didn't wear suits anymore. Now he wore shorts! And even though the Bali Majestic didn't have spear guns, Kyle thought it was a whole lot more exciting than the stuffy old hotel in New York City. Besides, nobody was bothered here if monkeys were around.

Kyle listened as his father greeted their special guest—Mr. Spalding. The big man scowled at Kyle, but his dog, Neil, yipped happily.

"Mr. Spalding," said Mr. Grant. "I cannot tell you how pleased we are that you've come to rate the Bali Majestic. My family and I are dedicated to making your stay at the Bali uneventful and trouble-free . . ."

Kyle wasn't really listening. He was too busy looking for Dunston. Finally he spotted his friend. Dunston sat at the top of a coconut tree! But he wasn't alone. A female orangutan sat next to Dunston—Mrs. Dunston! And in her arms she held a baby orangutan—Dunston, Jr.

But what Kyle noticed most was the coconut in Dunston's hand. The coconut that Dunston was getting ready to throw. To throw at Mr. Spalding!

"No!" cried Kyle. "Dunston! Not again!"

But Dunston just grinned as he wound up to toss the coconut. Why not have some fun? No matter what he did, Dunston knew his human family would always love him.